HOW I WONDER

GENERAL EDITOR

JACK BOOTH

DAVID BOOTH

WILLA PAULI & JO PHENIX

I M P R E S S I O N S

HOLT, RINEHART AND WINSTON OF CANADA, LIMITED

Sponsoring Editor: Sheba Meland
Senior Editor: Wendy Cochran
Production Editor: Jocelyn Van Huyse
Art Director: Wycliffe Smith
Design Assistant: Julia Naimska
Cover Illustrator: Heather Cooper

ISBN 0-03-921402-8

Canadian Cataloguing in Publication Data

Main entry under title:
How I Wonder

(Impressions)
For use in schools.
ISBN 0-03-921402-8

1. Readers (Primary). 2. Readers – 1950 –
I. Booth, Jack II. Series.

PE1119.H68   428.6   C83-098245-0

Illustrations
Frank Hammond: pp. 4-11, 12-13, 19-21; *Barbara Klunder*: pp. 14-15, 16-17; *Ilze Bertuss*: pp. 18, 80; *Joe Weissmann*: pp. 22-26; *John Burningham*: pp. 64-70; *Richard Bentham*: pp. 71-79; *Bijou Le Tord*: pp. 27-40; *Giulio Maestro*: pp. 41-53; *Rodney Peppé*: pp. 54-63.

The authors and publishers gratefully acknowledge the consultants listed below for their contribution to the development of this program:

Isobel Bryan   *Primary Consultant*   *Ottawa Board of Education*
Ethel Buchanan   *Language Arts Consultant*   *Winnipeg, Manitoba*
Heather Hayes   *Elementary Curriculum Consultant*   *City of Halifax Board of Education*
Gary Heck   *Curriculum Co-ordinator, Humanities*   *Lethbridge School District No. 51*
Ina Mary Rutherford   *Supervisor of Reading and Primary Instruction*   *Bruce County Board of Education*
Janice M. Sarkissian   *Supervisor of Instruction (Primary and Pre-School)*   *Greater Victoria School District*
Lynn Taylor   *Language Arts Consultant*   *Saskatoon Catholic School Board*

Acknowledgements
Sing a Rainbow: Words and Music by Arthur Hamilton. Copyright © 1955 Mark VII Music. All rights reserved. Used by permission of Edwin H. Morris (Canada) Limited. *Jelly in the Bowl*: From SALLY GO ROUND THE SUN by Edith Fowke reprinted by permission of The Canadian Publishers, McClelland and Stewart Limited, Toronto. *An Alphabet of Sounds*: Reprinted by permission of Four Winds Press, a division of Scholastic Inc. From AN ALPHABET OF SOUNDS by Bijou Le Tord. Copyright © 1981 by Bijou Le Tord. *Busy Day*: Reprinted from BUSY DAY by Betsy and Giulio Maestro. Text copyright © 1978 by Betsy Maestro. Illustrations copyright © 1978 by Giulio Maestro. By permission of Crown Publishers, Inc. *Henry's Exercises*: From HENRY'S EXERCISES by Rodney Peppé. Reprinted by permission of the publisher, Methuen Children's Books Ltd., London, England. *Would You Rather...*: Written and illustrated by John Burningham. Reprinted by permission of the publisher, Jonathan Cape Ltd. *Work Horses*: By Edith H. Newlin. From *Another Here and Now Story Book* by Lucy Sprague Mitchell. Copyright © 1937 by E.P. Dutton and Co., Inc. Renewal, 1965, by Lucy Sprague Mitchell. Reprinted by permission of the publisher, E.P. Dutton, Inc.

Care has been taken to trace the ownership of copyright material used in this text. The publishers will welcome any information enabling them to rectify any reference or credit in subsequent editions.

Printed in Canada   1 2 3 4   87 86 85 84

Table of Contents

Rainbow

by
David Booth

red

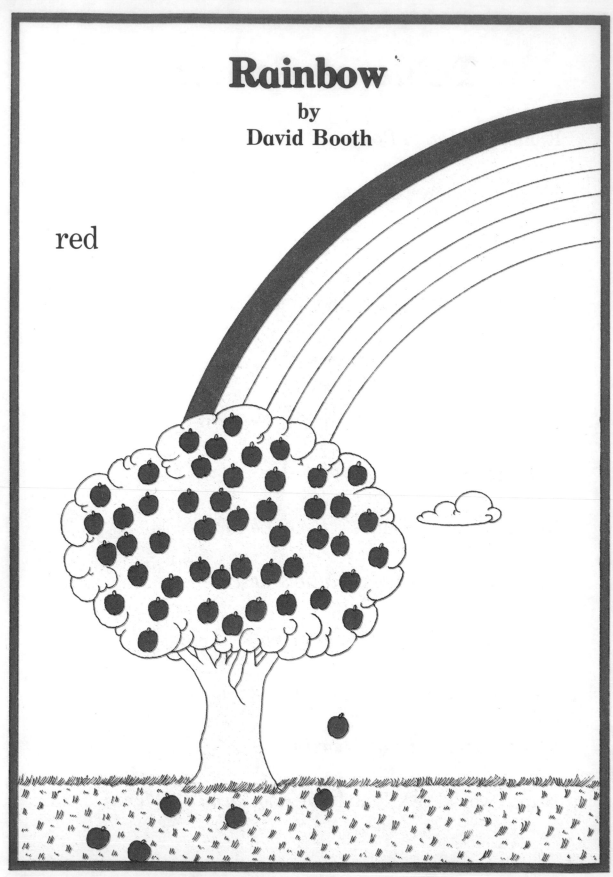

orange

yellow

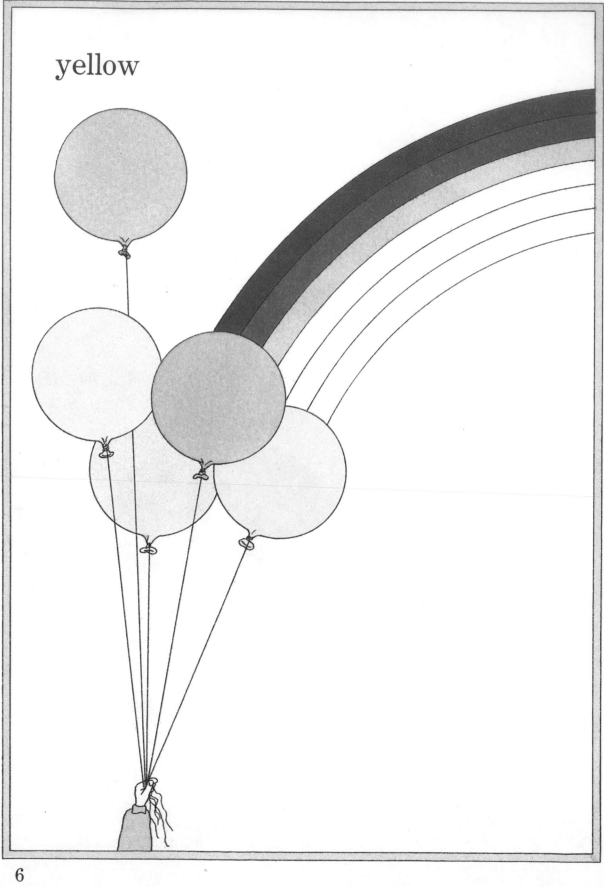

green

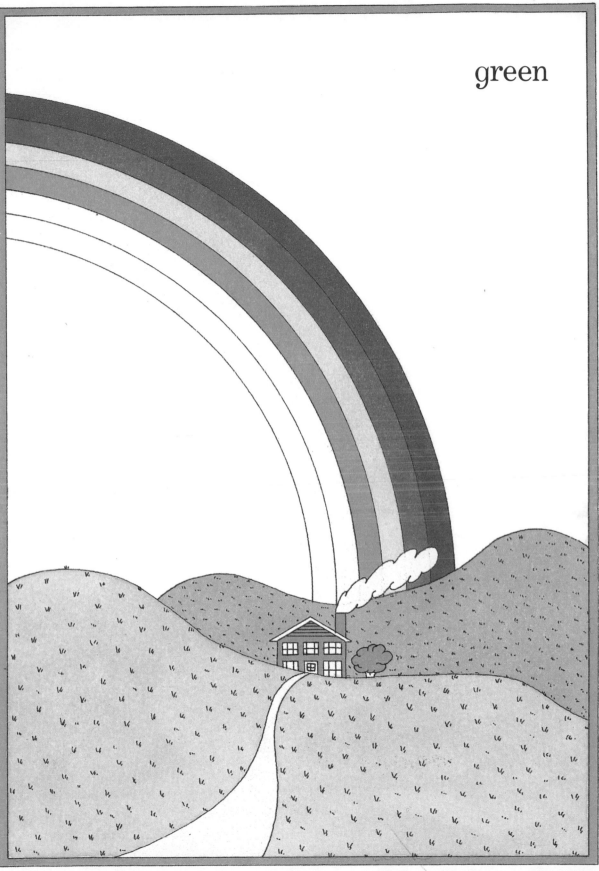

blue

purple

rainbow!

I can see a rainbow.
Can you?

Sing a Rainbow

by
Arthur Hamilton

Red and yellow and pink and green,
Purple and orange and blue,
I can sing a rainbow,
Sing a rainbow,
Sing a rainbow, too!

1,2, Buckle My Shoe
Traditional

1, 2,

Buckle my shoe,

3, 4,

Shut the door,

5, 6,
Pick up sticks,

7, 8,
Lay them straight,

9, 10,
A big fat hen.

One, Two, Bubblegum Chew

by
Meguido Zola

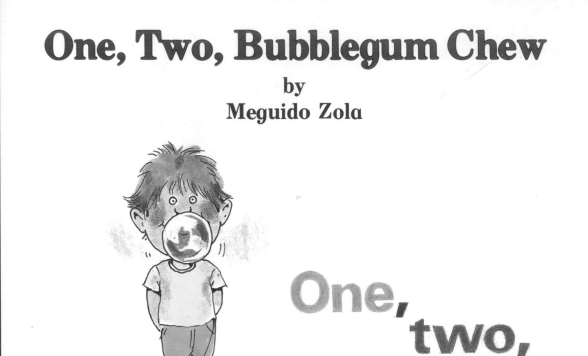

One,
two,

Bubblegum chew,

Three,
four,

Candy store,

Five, six,
Peppermint sticks,

Seven, eight,
Sticky date,

Nine, ten,
Start again.

Jelly in the Bowl
Traditional

Jelly in the bowl,
Jelly in the bowl,
Wibble wobble, wibble wobble,
Jelly in the bowl.

The More We Get Together
Traditional

The more we get together, together, together,
The more we get together, the happier we'll be.

'Cause your friends are my friends,
and my friends are your friends.

The more we get together,
the happier we'll be.

The Highway
by
David Booth

1 One highway
2 Two vans

5 Five race cars
6 Six jeeps

7 Seven tractor trailers
8 Eight pick-up trucks

9 Nine school buses
10 And ten little skunks.

26

An Alphabet of Sounds

by
Bijou Le Tord

A

achoo

arf arf

arf
arf
arf

a

B

buzz

baa

baa

boo

b

coo
coo

cluck
cluck

C

cheep cheep cheep

c

ding
ding ding
ding ding

D

dong
dong

d

29

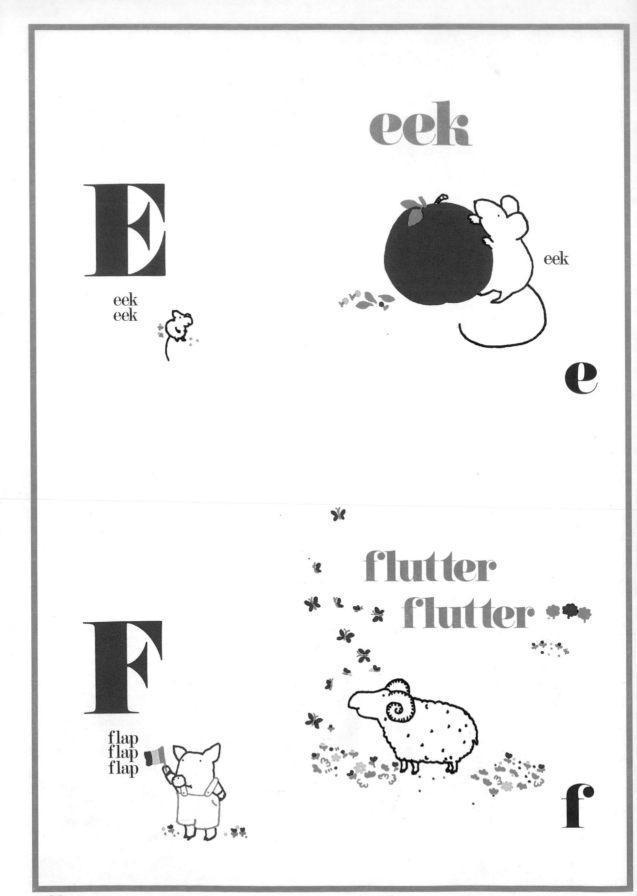

eek

E

eek
eek

eek

e

flutter
flutter

F

flap
flap
flap

f

grrr. growl

G

growl
growl

g

hee·haw

H

hoot hoot hoot

honk

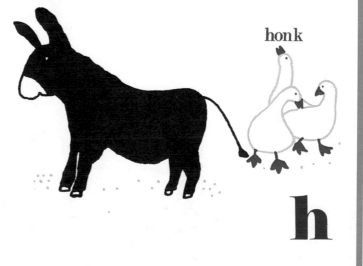

h

I

ick

ick

ick

i

J

jingle

jingle

jabber
jabber

j

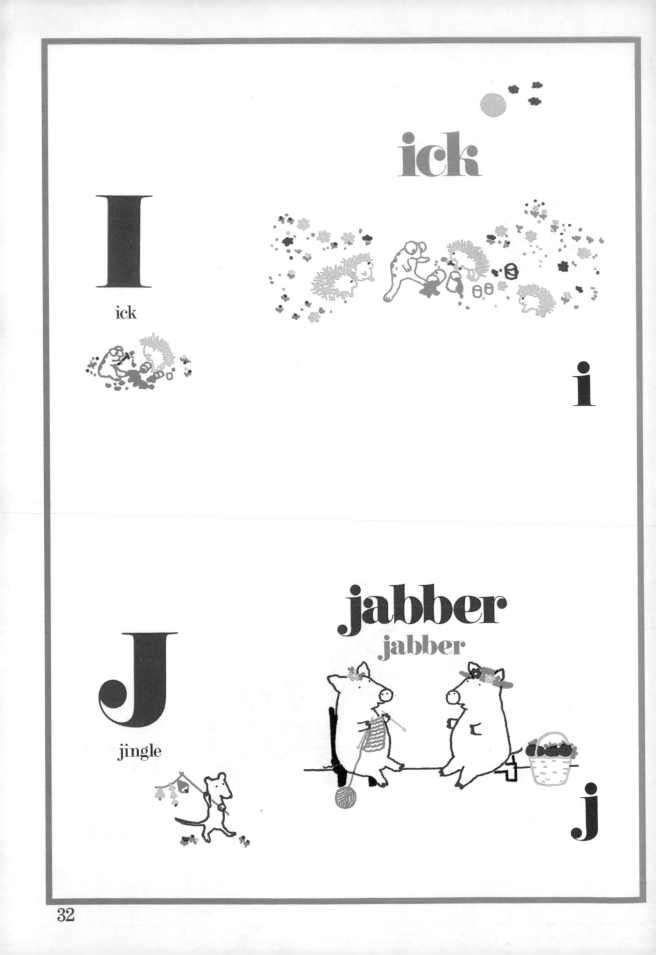

K

klunk
klunk
klunk

knock

k

L

la di da

la la la la la

la la la   l

moo

munch
munch

M

meow
meow
meow

m

neigh

N

neigh

n

oink
oink

O

oops

o

puff puff

putt·putt

P

purr purr

p

Q

quack
quack

quack

q

R

roar
roar
roar

roar
roar
roar

r

sniff
sniff

S

slurp
slurp

s

tick
tock
tick

T

tweet
tweet
tweet

t

37

ubble · gubble

U

ugh

u

vroom

V

vroom
vroom
vroom

v

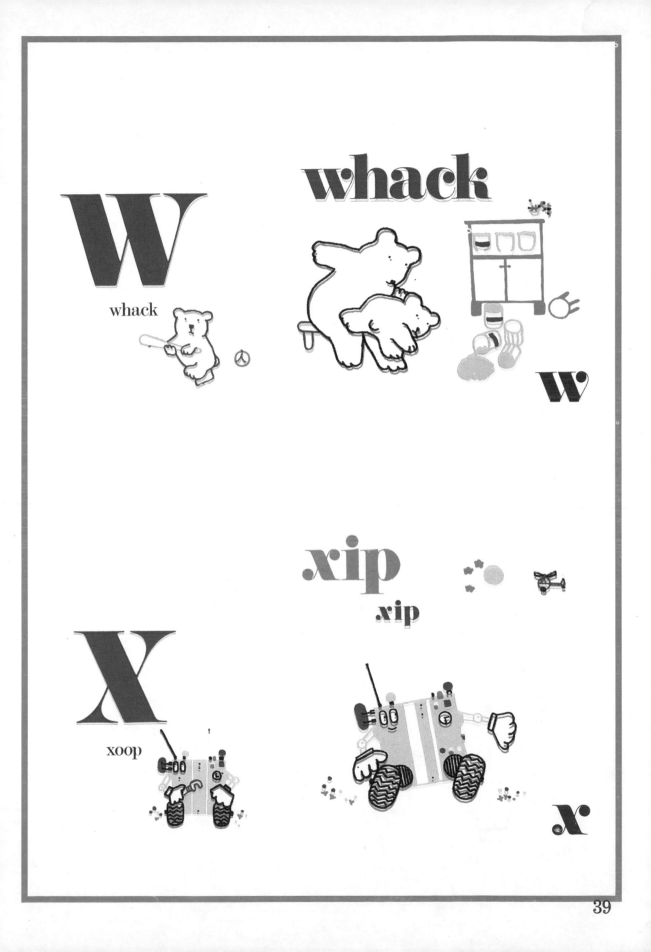

W

whack

whack

X

xoop

xip

xip

Y

yippee
yip

yay
yay
yay

y

Z

zap

Z
z
z
z

z

Busy Day
by
Betsy and Giulio Maestro

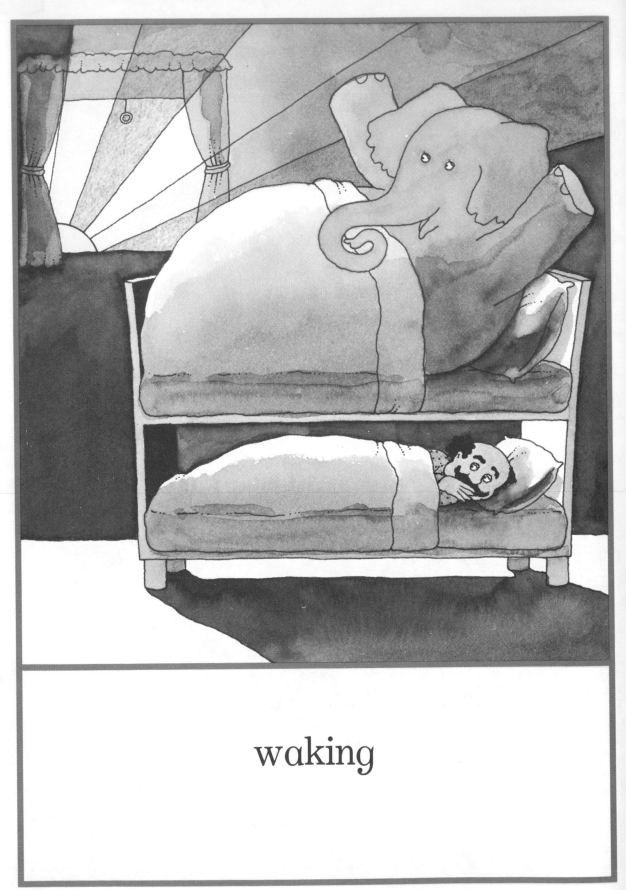

waking

washing

dressing

eating

working

painting

reading

sitting

swinging

jumping

dancing

waving

Henry's Exercises
by
Rodney Peppé

Henry is a toy elephant.
He sleeps in a shoe.

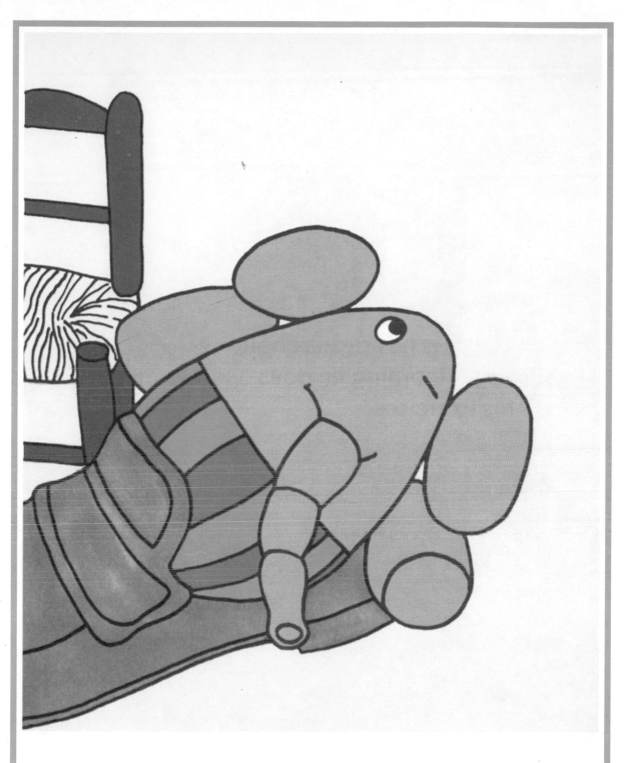

Henry is awake
and it is time to get up.

Henry is beside his chair.
Every morning
he does his exercises—

on the chair,

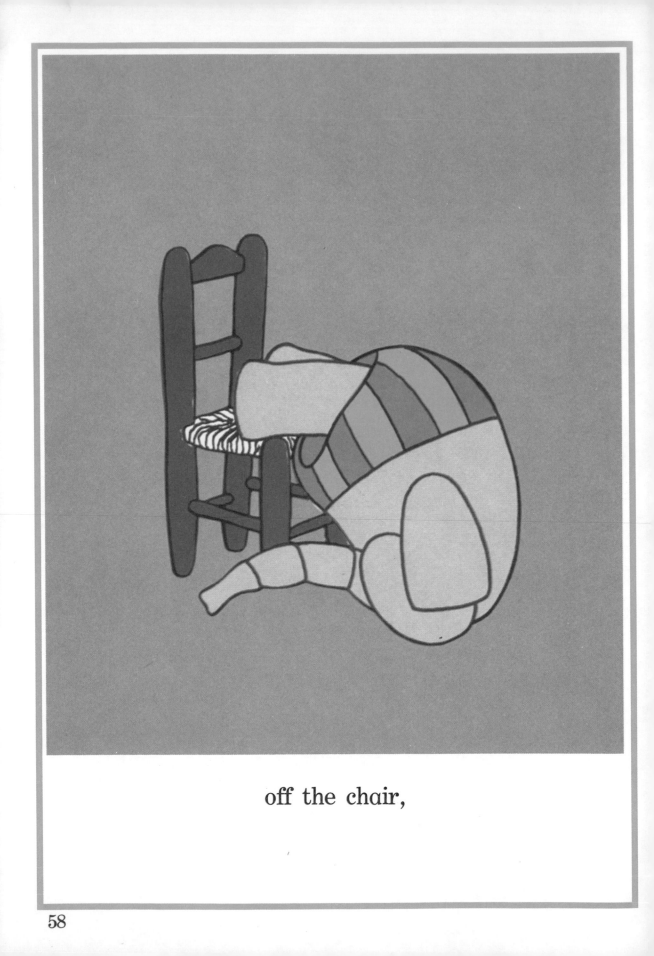

off the chair,

over the chair,

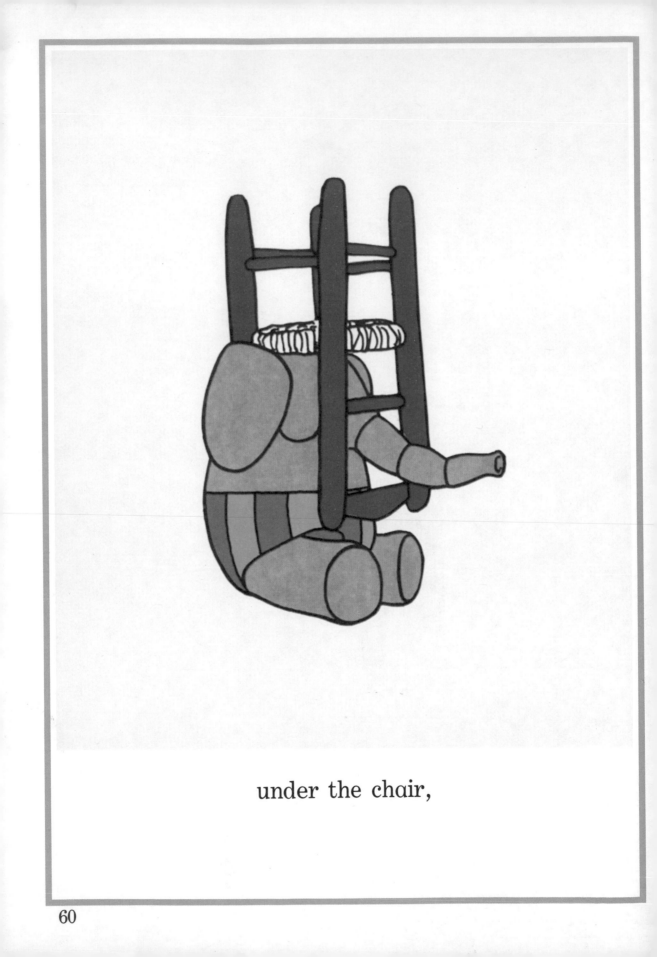

under the chair,

up the chair,

down the chair.

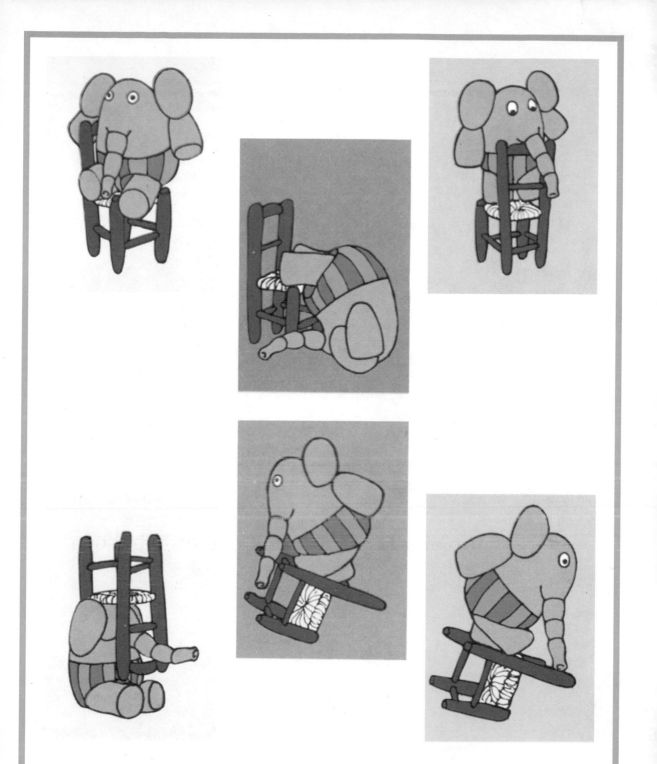

Every morning it is the same—
on, off, over, under,
up and down.

Would You Rather...
by
John Burningham

Would you rather have

supper in a castle,   breakfast in a balloon,

or tea on the river?

Would you rather be made to eat

spider stew,

slug dumplings,

mashed
worms,

or
drink
snail
pop?

Would you rather be

crushed by a snake,

swallowed by a fish,

eaten by a crocodile,

or sat on by a rhinoceros?

Would you rather have

a monkey to tickle,

a bear to read to,

a cat to box with,

a dog to skate with,

a pig to ride,

or a goat to dance with?

Or perhaps
you would rather
just go to sleep
in your own bed.

Work Horses
by
Edith Newlin

Big strong work horses
Working every day

Big strong work horses
Pulling loads of hay
work   work   work

Big strong work horses
Pull a wagon full

Big strong work horses
See them work and pull
pull   pull   pull

Big strong work horses
Digging up the ground

Big strong work horses
Walking round and round
walk   walk   walk

Big strong work horses
Going home to lunch

Eating oats, eating hay
See them munch and munch
munch   munch   munch

work work work

pull pull pull

walk walk walk

munch munch munch

Hup, Two, Three, Four!

by
Jack Booth and Jo Phenix

Hup, two, three, four!
Marching out
the palace door.
Five, six, seven, eight!
Sneaking past
the dragon's gate.
Hup, two, three, four!
"We'll catch you!"
the giants roar.
Five, six, seven, eight!
You won't see
us on a
giant's plate!